Rose Royal

ALSO BY NICOLAS MATHIEU

And Their Children After Them

ROSE ROYAL

A Love Story

Nicolas Mathieu

Translated from the French by Sam Taylor

OTHER PRESS

NEW YORK

Originally published in French as *Rose Royal* in 2019
by Éditions In8, Serres-Morlaàs, France

Copyright © Éditions In8 2019

English translation copyright © Sam Taylor 2022

Production editor: Yvonne E. Cárdenas
Text designer: Jennifer Daddio / Bookmark Design & Media Inc.
This book was set in Filosofia
by Alpha Design & Composition of Pittsfield, NH

1 3 5 7 9 10 8 6 4 2

LIBRARY OF CONGRESS CATALOGING-IN-PUBLICATION DATA
Names: Mathieu, Nicolas, 1978- author. | Taylor, Sam, 1970- translator.
Title: Rose Royal : a love story / Nicolas Mathieu ; translated from the French by Sam Taylor.
Other titles: Rose Royal. English
Description: New York : Other Press, [2022]
Identifiers: LCCN 2021033931 (print) | LCCN 2021033932 (ebook) |
ISBN 9781635421958 (hardcover) | ISBN 9781635421965 (ebook)
Subjects: GSAFD: Noir fiction. | LCGFT: Noir fiction. | Novellas.
Classification: LCC PQ2713.A8767 R6713 2022 (print) | LCC PQ2713.A8767 (ebook) |
DDC 843/.92—dc23
LC record available at https://lccn.loc.gov/2021033931
LC ebook record available at https://lccn.loc.gov/2021033932

PART ONE

ROSE JUMPED OFF the bus and hurried across the street, paying no attention to traffic, although it was dense in both directions. She was wearing a pale cotton skirt that day and a pretty top that showed off her shoulders. A black jacket was slung across her handbag, and her heels were an unmissably bright cherry red. From a distance, it was hard to guess her age, but the firmness of her figure and the fluidity of her movements suggested a certain youthfulness. Her legs, in particular, were still beautiful. Cars braked as she passed, causing a ripple in the smooth rush-hour flow, and a bearded man in a Ford Escort honked his horn for the sake of it. Rose didn't even notice. She continued on her way, feet moving quickly, indifferent to her surroundings. She took off her sunglasses and slipped them into her purse just as she was opening the door of the Royal. The clattering echo of her heels faded to silence as she entered the familiar darkness of her local bar. She checked her watch. It was still early. Rose felt happy. She was thirsty.

"Hi, everyone!"

"Hey," replied Fred, the owner.

While he poured her a beer, Rose opened the newspaper. She came here every day, on her way from work, and always sat at the bar, legs proudly crossed at the knees, to sink her first lager of the night. It was usually about seven o'clock when she got here. Often it was dark outside, except during summer, when Rose would feel a tinge of remorse.

The Royal was a narrow dive with dark walls and a long bar, three draft-beer pumps, and large, dusty bay windows offering a view of a Chinese restaurant, a shoe repair shop, and a convenience store. In the back they had foosball and pool. The furniture was from the seventies, in wood and blue leatherette. The restrooms were on the right as you went in; they were pretty clean, with stickers all over the walls. The atmosphere in the bar was eternally late-afternoon. The clientele could vary, but the music that came through the speakers was always rock.

As soon as she swallowed her first mouthful of beer, Rose felt something loosen inside her chest. The beer was cold, the pages of the newspaper were crumpled, and beneath her left shoe she could feel the solidity of the metal footrest. Those three sensations were enough to make her feel at home, in her place. She licked her finger to turn the page and Fred asked her what was happening.

She shrugged. "Same old same old."

Rose was almost fifty, but she didn't mind too much. She was aware of her attributes: her figure was still good and her legs were gorgeous. Her face, on the other hand, was showing signs of wear. It wasn't fat or especially gaunt, but time had left its mark of tears and sleepless nights. Her mouth was complicated by wrinkles. And her hair wasn't as thick and luxurious as it had been, part of that sensual abundance that had made her so attractive. She dyed it, so at least nobody could tell she was going gray.

She had reached that difficult age where what remains to you of youthful vigor and electricity seems to be vanishing under the rising tide of days. Sometimes, during a meeting or while traveling on public transport, she would find herself hiding her hands, which she no longer recognized. Certain evenings, looking in the mirror, she would tell her reflection, *Time to start taking better care of yourself.* At the supermarket, she'd spend a small fortune on creams and shampoos. Words like "firming," "cellulite," "hematite," and "collagen" had become part of her vocabulary. She'd enrolled in a water aerobics class and occasionally she would make a resolution to give up alcohol. She would also follow special diets based on vegetables, white meat, and nuts. But each time, she found herself surrendering to feelings of *Oh, what's the point?* It was a little late for this kind of stuff, wasn't it? Besides, it probably wouldn't make much difference.

Rose had married at twenty. She'd had two kids soon after that—Bastien and Grégory—and then a divorce without major complications. She'd had various bosses, adventures, symbolic promotions, health problems, meetings in the principal's office. These days she was entitled to an annual bonus and a company car—a white Fiat Punto that she hardly ever used. She lived in a rent-controlled apartment and her boys had found jobs and girlfriends. She slept badly and had stopped making plans for vacations. Sometimes it seemed like she was living her life on autopilot. Her happiest moments were always here, sitting at the bar, chatting with Fred, feeling the first glimmers of intoxication. And then there was her best friend, Marie-Jeanne, who came by on Tuesdays and Thursdays.

"Is she coming tonight?"

"Who?"

"Marie-Jeanne."

"Should be, yeah," said Fred.

"There's nobody here, though. She won't be happy."

"I've told her before she should make appointments. She never listens."

Twice a week the Royal was transformed into a hairdressing salon. Marie-Jeanne offered her services for ten euros a pop, and she had a drink between each customer, so it was always best to get your hair cut early in the evening. She and Rose had a lot in common: they were the same age, they were both sick of men, they'd brought up their kids single-handedly, and they felt like they were treading water and wished they weren't. Anyway they had nothing to be ashamed of. They'd both made it through good times and bad. And they had each other.

Rose finished her first glass and ordered another. A few more customers had turned up and she was in a happy mood. When Fred said something about the latest railway workers' strike bringing the country to a standstill yet again, Rose just rolled her eyes—proof that she was in good spirits. Marie-Jeanne finally arrived just after nine, as Rose was finishing her third beer.

"What happened to you?"

"Oh God, what a day! Traffic jams practically nonstop from Pompey to here. All those damn trucks..."

The hairdresser looked around for potential customers. It wasn't a busy night but it wasn't dead either. As always, Serge Kalt and the Keuss were downing beers at the end of the bar. Apart from them, it was the usual crowd of marginals, drunkards, aging punks, people who hated their jobs, and people who hadn't had a job in a long time. Nothing to write home about. Marie-Jeanne didn't hold out much hope for those thirtysomethings sitting at a table talking about architecture and drinking La Chouffe. And then there was that guy in glasses chatting up a woman ten years his junior. Sensing a Tinder date, Marie-Jeanne sighed.

"Nothing but hipsters and hoboes . . . I bet you I don't make a cent tonight."

"There's still time."

"Yeah . . . I'm not going to be cutting hair at two in the morning, though, am I?"

Marie-Jeanne ordered a pastis to drown her sorrows and grabbed the newspaper from the countertop.

"I don't believe it. After all this time! God, I'm so sick of reading about this story . . ."

She slapped the newspaper's front page with the back of her hand, indicating another headline about the Grégory Affair. Thirty years after the murder, Jacqueline and Marcel Jacob were being questioned, while Murielle Bolle was finally going to speak out. Rose still remembered the first photograph appearing in *L'Est Républicain* one October morning. A gendarme carrying the child's body, little Grégory's hat pulled down over his face, his hands and feet tied together. She saw the boy's tiny shoes again, size 9s at a guess. Five hours before that, the poor kid had still been playing with his toy cars on a pile of sand in his parents' backyard. And suddenly there he was, skin like ice in the glare of the flash, a little boy turned to meat. When the story began, Bastien must have been about five, the same age as the victim, more or less. Like many people in the area, Rose had followed each episode with growing avidity. Of course the crime horrified her.

But there was something else, something deeper. She recognized those people. She'd grown up in the Meuse, in a family of the same type, relationships pockmarked with silences and grudges, a small town in the back of beyond, with two factories and houses lined up across narrow streets, a town full of prejudices and animosities that went back to the Occupation. She understood the way those people moved, the way they kept quiet about things, the heavy accents, the stubbornly shaking heads. The journalists made fun of them, but those people existed. They were the country's cannon fodder, the lifeblood of its factories, they were the masses who watched television and didn't vote, the crowds at funfairs, the reality of society. Rose hated the way they were portrayed in the media. She wouldn't have said anything either, in their shoes. It wasn't anyone else's business. But still . . . that poor kid. She imagined how cold his hands must have been, his waterlogged anorak, his black hair and pale skin, and her throat tightened.

After her second pastis, Marie-Jeanne started to grow impatient. The idea that she had come all this way for nothing drove her crazy. She needed to work, at least enough to pay for her gas, and in the end she fell back on Rose.

"Come on, I'll trim your ends. Half-price."

"No, no way."

"Seriously, look, they're splitting."

"Leave my hair alone. I don't want you wrecking it with your scissors."

"Just a quick trim. It'll only take a few seconds."

Rose kept saying no, but soon she found herself sitting in the middle of the room facing a full-length mirror that Marie-Jeanne lugged around with her everywhere she went, a towel over her shoulders, while her friend's hands fluttered around her head.

"You're cutting it too short..."

"Don't worry. You won't even notice the difference."

There was no point arguing. While she waited Rose eyed her reflection and felt the same fast-fading surprise as always. She was not particularly vain and did not suffer from the melancholy that afflicted women for whom aging came as a sort of betrayal. But she did keep an image of herself somewhere deep inside, and the mirror's contradiction of this came, each time, as an unpleasant reality check. Marie-Jeanne kept working confidently, indifferently, while the drinkers who had briefly shown an interest in the spectacle soon went back to their conversations. Rose was left alone with the mirror's observations on the passing of time. The idea amused her and she smiled to herself. After all, she was proud of her own unflinching gaze, her ability to stare at her reflection without telling herself lies, without pretending or denying the facts or dreaming up consolations like so many of the women she knew. At least she could be glad about one thing. The trials she'd been through had rewarded her with the unquestionable gift of her own resilience. Rose was a strong woman now. You only had to see the way she handled herself with men.

The last guy she'd gone out with for any length of time was luckier than he realized; he'd had a narrow escape. A balding man in his forties, Thierry worked for an energy services company and divided his spare time between his blended family, his Netflix subscription, and his local cycling club, which had been planning a hypothetical ride up to the Col du Galibier for the past two years. He was a quiet, considerate man. Not particularly good-looking but at least he wouldn't hurt a fly. Or so she'd thought until one night when he was watching the news and Rose was talking on the phone and he'd told her to shut her mouth because he couldn't hear what the anchorman was saying. After that they'd got into a muddled dispute, with the TV blaring in the background, and at one point Rose had sensed that Thierry was close to raising his hand to her. She'd recognized that tension in his face, the ugliness of men whose arguments have run dry. It was always the same old story. You touched the nerve of his pride and his fist came down on you. In the end Thierry had just stormed out, slamming the door behind him.

After he'd left, Rose had not been able to do anything for a while. But she hadn't cried. Then she'd got in the car and driven up to the Plateau de Brabois to take her mind off things. It was a clear night and the cold, bracing air had made her feel better. She'd made her decision. The next day she would buy a small revolver from an American website, a .38 caliber, five rounds, 650 euros. It was a lot of money, and that in itself told a story.

After an eleven-day wait, the gun was delivered to a nearby pickup point. She tore off the bubble-wrap and was stunned by the object's almost supernatural beauty. It was silver and black, plump and incredibly solid. She watched YouTube videos on how to handle the gun, then took it out to some woods on the edge of town. The first shot made her heart pound like a first date. Even after that, she barely got used to it. Rose had not been an especially good shot and had made no real attempt to improve. She'd just made sure that she could keep her hand still when she fired it. The main thing was that she wouldn't look ridiculous pointing that thing at a man's face. Fear had to switch sides.

For weeks she'd waited for Thierry to yell at her again. It was exciting. She imagined his face, his barking, and then the look in his eyes when she aimed the revolver's black muzzle at him. We'd see where the balance of power was then. She'd known her share of bastards, thugs, and morons. Very few of them had dared to really hit her. But all of them—because they were stronger than her, always angry, and because they felt they had the right—had made her submit to their will. The revolver would enable her to put a stop to this cycle. She was determined. She'd pull the trigger if she had to.

With Thierry, however, nothing had happened. One day he'd just stopped coming around, stopped calling her. After two months of being together, he simply vanished from her life. Another bastard, then, but not the kind that deserved to die.

Since then, she had taken the .38 with her everywhere, a heavy weight in her purse, a helpful presence, a true companion. Through watching more videos, she'd also learned to clean it. Sometimes, at night in her kitchen, she would stare at it cradled in her white hands. She'd bought it secondhand and she wondered if it had ever been fired before. She wondered if that tough, squat, bulldoglike object had ever killed a man. She picked it up and pointed it at the glass oven door, which offered her a thrilling glimpse of her reflection: a homicidal woman. She squeezed the trigger, her index finger trembled, then the hammer rose and snapped shut again with a cold, metallic click. A delicious frisson ran through her shoulders, throat, and breasts. This acquisition undoubtedly marked a turning point in her life. She wondered what had taken her so long, because she had a history of ambiguous relationships with men that went way back. To her father, if she really thought about it. Love had been mixed with fear from the beginning. She'd fooled around with her cousins and then, at about thirteen, her body had started to change: first her legs, then her ass, her tits, the whole shebang. After that, her existence had really been centered on boys. She'd never tried to keep count, but she certainly hadn't been bored. She'd sought boys out and submitted to them, both at once.

Years later, when Rose ate lunch with her parents on Saturdays, it had been strange to hear her mother say things like *That Humbert girl's been with every man in town*, or *She's like a woman possessed, that one*. If only she'd known... Rose ate a bit more gratin and thought about those long-lost dates, in the backseats of freezing cars or lying on the ground near the soccer field amid the mingled odors of earth and wet grass. She remembered wandering hands, stolen pleasures, burning desires. And stupid pricks who didn't understand that no means no. Back then she'd always blamed herself. If she wanted to get it on, she had to pay for the pleasure in the currency of risk. On two different occasions she'd got a smack for her troubles and the guy had pulled down her panties and done his business quickly, unpleasant but brief. Afterward he'd dropped her at home, they'd both said bye, she hadn't made a fuss. Alone in her room, Rose hadn't thought, *I've been raped*. She hadn't thought anything at all. She'd cried into her pillow and groggily fallen asleep without even removing her makeup. A week later her thoughts had moved on. And yet it remained there constantly, like tinnitus, an endless humming sound.

That evening at the Royal, Marie-Jeanne had very few customers but she didn't have time to dwell on this at any length because, around eleven p.m., a dozen high schoolers came in, pretty far gone, undoubtedly too young to drink, and very loud and happy. They were all in costume, their faces covered by makeup or flour.

"Whoa!" said Fred when he saw them massing at the bar. "What the hell's going on?"

"Innkeeper!" shouted one young guy in an orange wig, slamming his hand on the countertop. "We're thirsty!"

"Yeah, well, we're about to close...Hey! Did you hear me?"

It turned out that the kids—seniors at a local private school—had been celebrating the "Percent," the day one hundred days before their baccalaureate exams began. They'd been roaming the town since morning, drinking, throwing confetti all over the roads, and getting half-heartedly chased by the cops. Their day of fun was reaching its end. Tomorrow they would be back to the daily grind: studying, eyes on the prize, badgered by their parents to succeed. But before they succumbed to this fate, they wanted one last drink. They'd agreed to pool their money and they were piling it up now on the counter.

"I said we're closing," Fred repeated, holding out his hands and pretending to shove them out into the street,

"Come on, sir!"

"We can pay!"

"That's not the issue."

Fred tapped his watch, intransigent. It was closing time—end of story. Leaning on the bar, Rose and Marie-Jeanne watched with softhearted indulgence as this scene unfolded. A pudgy girl with bleached-blond hair stared at them in a daze. Marie-Jeanne decided to take matters into her own hands.

"All right, listen, drinks for everyone!" she declared.

"What?" asked Fred in a panic.

And the kids chorused: "Drinks for everyone!"

Then they began roaring, banging their fists on the bar or the tables, and stamping their feet on the floor, rallying the last few customers to their cause. Gradually, the teenagers' enthusiasm won over the others. Marie-Jeanne stuck her fingers in her mouth and whistled.

"Hey!" Everyone fell silent and turned toward her. Looking very serious and pointing one index finger in the air like a teacher, she said, "One drink and that's it. Okay?"

There was general support for this suggestion. Money was handed over. Beer flowed. And the conversations started up again, way louder than before. The teenagers mingled with the regulars. They talked about everything and nothing. No one was really listening. But that last drink was quickly downed and soon the drinkers were begging Fred for another. The bartender began to fume. The cops could turn up at any moment and take his license. They were already giving him a hard time over noise levels and people selling weed on his premises. Everybody had to leave now.

"Oh, come off it," said Rose, who by now was pretty wasted. "Why would the cops come here? Especially on a Thursday..."

"It's late, I'm tired, we're closing. That's it."

"Come on Fred, we're actually having a laugh for once!"

Grudgingly he started handing out plastic glasses and took his own box of Côtes-du-Rhône from its hiding place under the bar. It was already half-empty so it wouldn't last long. This seemed like a good compromise.

"After this, *basta!*" Fred swore. "Whatever happens, I'm closing."

The wine was mauve-colored with an acidic taste that attacked your tongue and left you even thirstier. They made several new toasts, most of them to the bartender's health. It became more and more difficult for him to maintain his bad mood. Then the Keuss started singing and the others half-listened. Once upon a time he'd been in a local rock band that had mostly done covers of Depeche Mode and Indochine. In the late eighties they'd released an album containing twelve songs of their own, which sold about two hundred copies. Rose could still remember the sleeve. Back then, the Keuss had been blessed with beautiful hair and had worn a black tank top that showed off his pale, wiry arms, a line of kohl under each eye giving him that sexually ambivalent New Wave look. Thirty years later he was a fat man with a scratchy voice, his shirt front opened to reveal his hairless chest, bellowing, "Death to the cops, death to the pigs!" Sitting on her barstool, legs crossed, plastic glass raised to her lips, Rose thought how distant their youth seemed.

The festivities went on amid a cheerfully amnesiac disorder. The kids were in no rush to get home, the adults even less so. From time to time Rose would glance over at the clock on the wall and think, *Oh well*. The evening had imperceptibly morphed into a full-on fiesta and alcohol had enveloped everything in its aura of perpetual now. The only place that still offered any clarity was the restroom. When Fred agreed to open another wine box there was a huge cheer and everything seemed possible. Hell, maybe they could keep this going until dawn...

Then something smashed outside. The drinkers stared at each other. It was nothing precise, a snag in the fabric of the moment, but thirty bodies froze, all their joy instantly swept away. The seconds passed stark and heavy, like drops of water falling into a metal sink. Everyone was waiting, tensed, for whatever would happen next, thinking without daring to say it out loud about the Bataclan and all those other impossible events that transformed places of pleasure into slaughterhouses. Finally one of the teenage boys said, "What was that? Did you hear it?"

"Must be a car," said Fred.

Immediately, as if to prove him right, an engine roared in the next street over. Inside the bar the drinkers smiled, relieved to hear this thunderous growl, this ordinary, easily identifiable, almost natural noise. They listened to it grow louder and then gradually fade as it disappeared down Avenue Jeanne d'Arc toward the southbound highway.

"V-8," proclaimed an expert.

"Wish I had one of those," said someone else.

The customers did not have time to dwell on this subject, however, because just then the door of the Royal opened to reveal a man holding some sort of soft, shape-less form in his arms. At first they thought it must be a cloth or a towel, heavy with water, dripping on the floor. The man took two steps forward and their stomachs were suddenly tied in knots. Someone moaned.

"Oh my God," said Marie-Jeanne, grabbing Rose by the arm.

The shape was actually an animal. A dog, broken, its head hanging limp. Blood streamed from its open mouth. Its ribcage fluttered as it panted quickly. The man came farther into the bar and the animal whined. He was hold-ing the body up at chest level so that everyone could see it. As if he wanted the people in the bar to bear witness.

"What happened?" Marie-Jeanne asked.

It was almost a rhetorical question. Given the situ-ation, there wasn't much room for mystery on that score. All around, the drinkers' inebriation was ebbing and their faces were taking on expressions of sorrow and embar-rassment. The man holding the dog was tall with sparse, short-cut hair, and the front of his shirt was soaked with blood. He knelt down and placed the poor beast on the tiled floor. There was an almost disturbing gentleness to every movement he made. The animal was still panting. Its black liquid eye rolled around, seeking out faces.

"What happened?" repeated Marie-Jeanne, who had moved closer.

She too knelt down, and reached out toward the dog whose pretty pointed ears were now lowered. But the man held her wrist to prevent her touching the animal. Marie-Jeanne looked at his gaunt, vertical face but could read nothing in his expression but a sort of suppressed effort. His mouth was half-open and she could see his long, tobacco-yellowed incisors. One of them was slightly crooked and this flaw, by contrast, gave the rest of his face a strange rubbery density.

"She was run over by a car."

There was something impossible about this whole scene. The kneeling man, the drunkenness and pallid light of the Royal, the terrible silence in the street, the dying animal, that hand holding a wrist. In the end the man let go of Marie-Jeanne and she realized that he'd hurt her. Rose went over there too and felt her heart rise to the base of her throat. On the floor the dog's insides were starting to seep out: blood, organs, a wet-colored chaos of vile, sloppy guts still quivering with the remnants of life.

"We should call the cops," someone said.

Nobody did.

"She's in pain," said the man.

The poor beast remained motionless, ever more docile, its body rippled by rapid, agonized breaths. The man didn't dare touch it. Once again he reminded everyone that the dog was in pain.

"What should we do?" asked Rose.

"There's nothing we can do," said the man. "She's going to die."

Less than two minutes had passed since he'd entered the bar, but it felt much longer than that. The teenagers looked like they'd been up all night and some of them were eyeing the exit. Fred came over and stood above the eviscerated body. And he thought he'd seen everything before.

"What's her name?"

"Lola."

The man gently stroked the dog's dark fur. He had beautiful hands. Beneath his skin, you could see the movements of tendons, the roll of the blue veins. The animal hiccupped and threw up a bit of blood. Somewhere behind them, a girl started sobbing.

"We can't just leave her like this," said Marie-Jeanne.

Rose agreed. She went back to the bar, where she'd left her purse. She opened it, glanced inside, and took out the revolver. Around her, people edged backward while emitting a sort of soft, disapproving murmur. But they didn't have time to react more than that. Rose was already standing over the dog. She aimed the barrel at its head, fired, and that was that.

Of course everyone there had heard hundreds of gunshots on TV before. This one seemed disappointing in comparison. It was just a quiet, nasal crack, although it left their ears numb afterward. On the floor, the animal was no longer breathing. A dark red halo was spreading around its head. The man gave the dog a final caress between the ears, lifted his hand, and looked up at Rose. With a nod, he thanked her.

His name was Luc.

PART TWO

I N THE END things had moved pretty fast. Two days after the incident at the Royal, she'd received a call. She was reading *Paris Match* in the dentist's waiting room when her cell phone started to ring.

"Hello?"

"It's Luc."

At the time his name had meant nothing. In her lap the magazine was showing off its latest installment of predictable photographs. There was a long story about Emmanuel and Brigitte Macron, and the pictures looked like they'd been taken from a photo album of someone's vacation. Rose wasn't really interested in politics but she liked this new president because he was young, self-assured, and still in love with his wife. It made a change from all those losers who had only one ambition as soon as they hit their forties: dump their kids' mother and move in with some young floozy with a flat stomach. She and Marie-Jeanne had affectionately nicknamed the First Lady "Bribri." They talked about her as if she were a reality TV star. And at least that odd couple was a distraction from other, less acceptable political truths. The Macrons were good-looking and well-bred, and Rose made do with that.

"Luc who?"

"You don't remember? It was my dog who got run over the other night."

Rose felt a burst of heat rise from her stomach up to her cheeks. Without asking the other patients in the room she opened the window to let in some air, then went to a corner to continue her conversation away from prying ears. Luc wanted to see her again. "Why not," she said. When the dentist came to fetch her, she was still staring into space.

That first time, Luc invited her for a drink on Place Stan', an old classic. It was a warm evening in May and they were both dressed to the nines, feeling tongue-tied and a little idiotic surrounded by successful fifty-somethings and brain-dead teenagers.

"I haven't done this for a while," Luc admitted.

"Me neither."

Rose was not being completely honest. The previous winter, tired of sleeping alone in her double bed, she'd created accounts on a couple of dating sites, Adopte and Meetic. They were free for women and all you had to do was post a photograph, fill in your profile—I like traveling, food, spending time with family, and the movies of Louis de Funès—and then set out your expectations. Rose had written: "I'm looking for a man who's open-minded, available, at least six feet tall (I like to wear heels), who loves nature, animals, lazy Sunday mornings in bed, going to see a good movie or having a drink on a café terrace. No womanizers, married men, or other losers."

After perfecting her profile she'd spent a few evenings in front of her computer instead of going to the Royal, although she did arm herself with a bottle of port so she wouldn't feel lonely. It was funny seeing all those guys scrolling past on the screen. Short ones, dark ones, bald ones, young ones, lots of them posing in front of their car or bare-chested, almost all of them morons, pervs with gel in their hair, eternal bachelors, and the vast majority also illiterate, incapable of a single original thought or even of using an apostrophe correctly, desperate for sex and willing to do just about anything to sleep with a woman in full working order. And that was it: take your pick. Any man who liked the look of you would send you a charm or a heart or whatever name that particular site gave to a digital request, and then, if you were up for it, he could send you a message. Two times out of three Rose would bring the conversation to an end as soon as he wrote "how ya doin?" or paid her a compliment that had obviously been copied and pasted a thousand times before. But occasionally a presentable guy would pop up. And the two of you could start to chat. Shyly at first. Then, loosened by a few glasses of port, she would grow bolder. During these remote conversations Rose had laughed a lot and even touched herself a little bit in bed.

Despite her age, plenty of men had wanted to meet her, which was ultimately quite reassuring and flattering. But overall the world of online dating had left an unpleasant taste in her mouth. If you were sex-starved nowadays it was not from a lack of choice or opportunities. What people wanted was love, passion, a soul mate, almost impossible to find and consequently monetized. Because everyone was alone, their time monopolized by work, by their busy, productive lives. They were all divorced at forty, addicted to fucking, to their screens, uprooted to unknown cities, eaten away by a need for constant change that extended to their romantic lives, and in the end they spent their evenings on the computer, tapping away late at night in bed, hoping to be saved by a hypothetical hot date. All those innumerable solitary existences, numbed by online spending frenzies and TV dinners, were the very fabric of modernity and the networks it spawned. They were the gold deposits of our time. It was from this mass of separation and suffering that Big Tech made its fortune. Billions of dollars were milked from this worldwide woe.

Rose had gone on a few dates, all of them disappointing. Yet, apart from one firefighter who thought he had a right to sex because he'd paid for a meal and a bottle of Boulaouane at the local couscous restaurant, all those men had been relatively kind and sweet. Exactly what she wanted, on paper. The only problem was . . . they bored her stiff. As soon as they began talking about their job, their ex-wife, or their kids, as soon as they asked her what she liked to do in her spare time, Rose's mind would start to wander. She would feel desperately thirsty. She'd finish her glass and immediately want another one. "Sorry, I have to go." The poor guy would hear her say, "It was nice, I'm just tired" as she shook his hand and then he'd watch her walk away, hips swaying atop those beautiful legs, a damaged and sexy woman. Stupid bitch.

Rose had soon put an end to it. Her digital profiles continued to exist without her. From time to time she'd get a notification in her in-box. Charlizangel visited your profile. Denis54 sent you a heart. How sad . . .

With Luc, on the other hand, something had happened almost instantly. Not that he was particularly chatty. And Rose hadn't made any effort to keep the conversation going. She just knew as soon as she looked at him. The people we like always seem familiar, somehow, like an old knickknack on a shelf. He was taller than she remembered, thin but with broad shoulders. And he had very heavy hands, worker's hands, worn by use, that stirred her heart. She wondered how old he might be. Probably close to fifty. His hair was mostly gray but it was cut so short that you couldn't really tell. There were purplish little veins visible on his cheeks and the sides of his nose, which gave him a good complexion as long as you didn't look too close. He wore jeans and a black polo shirt, forgettable shoes, and there was nothing about his appearance that allowed you to get a clear idea of his occupation, whether he made decent money or none at all. You could see that his clothes weren't new, though. After a while he got up from his chair and sat next to her. That way he, too, could enjoy observing the ebb and flow of humanity on the square.

"I like watching people."

"Yeah, me too. It's talking to them that I find more of a pain."

Rose smiled. She'd always had a soft spot for grumpy, difficult men. Her father had been like that. Her brother too. At least you always knew where you stood with them.

Later they felt hungry and Luc had to dig out his half-moon glasses to read the menu. Rose chose a salad, as she always did when she wanted to make a good impression.

"Wouldn't you rather have a steak? It's kind of sad, don't you think, eating salads all the time . . ."

So they ordered two rare steaks with fries and a bottle of Syrah. They ate with a good appetite and drank without haste. After finishing his plate, Luc began dipping into the bread basket. It was soon empty.

"I tend to stuff myself when I'm nervous."

"So I see."

"I haven't even asked you about your life."

"Pfft!" Rose replied, waving her hand evasively.

All the same he made her describe to him exactly what she did as the executive assistant in an accounting firm. As for Luc, he just told her, "I do a bit of DIY."

It took Rose a couple of weeks to work out what this meant. In fact, Luc bought properties that nobody wanted—old apartments, dilapidated shop premises—and converted them into luxury lofts or four-bedroom houses. He had two employees whom he paid almost exclusively off the books. He drove an Audi Q6. His official job title was real estate agent.

After dinner, which Luc paid for in cash, they took a walk through the old downtown. He kept his hands in his pockets while she clung to her purse strap. The cobbled streets were full of tipsy youngsters, the café terraces were packed, and their footsteps echoed in the narrow medieval alleys. They took their time and didn't talk much. The evening air was an invitation to idleness. After a while they spotted something and the same idea popped into both of their heads. They felt like a drink.

"We could just go for a beer and afterward I'll take you home."

"I didn't want to ask but..."

They found a small bar, out of the way, near the Porte Désilles, with two tables out on the sidewalk and a foosball table in the back. They ordered half pints of Stella; it barely even counted as alcohol.

"Just one drink and then home."

"Cheers."

"Cheers."

After the first round, they kept ordering more. Luc and Rose were good drinkers. They didn't make any comment on how much they were consuming. They didn't suddenly start having a good time, their inhibitions blown away by intoxication. They didn't argue about the bill. They didn't talk to the other customers. They just drank their drinks and got to know each other. Soon they were saying *tu* instead of *vous*. They talked about Luc's dog. They talked about Rose's revolver.

"So you always carry that thing around with you?"

"More or less."

"What for?"

"To defend myself."

Luc frowned but didn't say anything. In the end it was Rose who restarted the conversation. Something had been bothering her since that night at the Royal.

"Lola's a strange name for a dog, don't you think?"

"It was my wife's idea."

"Oh, you were married?"

"Yeah."

"For a long time?"

"More than twenty years. She lives quite near here, in fact. With one of my oldest friends."

"Ah, that's weird!"

As is often the case with these things, they ended up finding they had loads in common. They both lived alone; they liked being able to have a few drinks without being criticized for it and having the whole bed to themselves. They both thought it was wrong to want to travel all over the world when the country where they lived was so beautiful. They both enjoyed hiking, watching old movies with Jean Gabin or Lino Ventura, and wished the long-running documentary series, *Thalassa*, about the sea, was still on every week instead of just once a month, given how most of the shows on TV these days were such crap. They reminisced about the blackboards and the white smocks they used to wear at school, and they shared the foreboding that the kids of today would all end up morons from spending so much time on screens. They'd both been on the left before giving up on politics altogether. They'd both had kids who were now grown up and who only called them two or three times a year—on New Year's Eve, Mother's Day, or Father's Day, that kind of crap. After getting divorced they'd both looked for a new partner, without much success, and in retrospect

their fumbling attempts had become a source of hilar-
ity, each failure transformed into an anecdote that made
their friends laugh. They'd both accepted that all that
stuff was behind them now, and that they just had to keep
going and make the best of things. And yet here they
were, looking deep into each other's eyes, living proof
that they'd been wrong to give up.

It was true that Luc wasn't very talkative and Rose
had to shoulder the burden of keeping their conversation going. But she was used to that, and all in all she
preferred it to being stuck with some smooth-talking
fake. At the end of the evening it was Luc who made the
first move, inviting her for one last drink at his place.
He lived about twelve miles out of the center of town,
but Rose accepted anyway and they both got into his im-
pressive gray sedan. Despite being well over the limit,
Luc drove home without apparent difficulty and without
worrying about the cops or speed traps either. Like many
guys of his type, he believed some laws did not apply to
him. This belief encompassed all laws relating to his car,
as well as those concerned with alcohol, tobacco, social
security payments, and income tax. The powerful car
glided smoothly along the zigzagging roads that led to
Luc's house, lighting up the darkness with its white eyes
and giving an impression of absolute safety and privilege
to which Rose very quickly grew accustomed. Not only

that, but when they turned on the radio the first song that came on was "Requiem pour un fou" by Johnny Hallyday, one of her favorites—surely a good sign. She listened to it in silence, gazing into the distance, prey to that delicious suspense that always accompanies the first time. She wondered what his place would be like...

She wasn't disappointed. Luc lived in an old, isolated, L-shaped farmhouse. He'd renovated it at great expense and installed large bay windows in the walls, flooding the high-ceilinged rooms with daylight—or with the darkness of the night, as was the case just then. A white gravel driveway bisected a perfect green lawn that sloped down to an orchard full of mirabelle plum trees. Beyond that, a line of taller trees shielded them from the rest of the world. It was easy to believe that the neighbors didn't exist at all. As she got out of the Audi, Rose shivered.

"Are you cold?"

"A little bit."

"Come inside."

They went through the garage. When they got into the living room, Luc asked her what she would like to drink. He stood in front of her, looking neither shy nor particularly passionate. Rose was no longer so sure of his intentions. He was a handsome man, she thought. She felt eager and afraid.

"Just water for me."

"Sparkling?"

"Yes, that's fine."

Luc poured himself a Coke with ice and, sitting side by side, they drank their drinks, uncertain how to begin. Rose thought about her belly and her breasts, which he was going to see. She dreaded that white flash of nudity. She had a certain routine when it came to bringing men home. A kiss in the living room, then she'd lead them into her bedroom, where the lampshades softened the lighting. She would strip them and suck them for a bit before taking off her own clothes. What happened after that was always fragmentary, confused, blurred amid the darkness, the sheets, and their movements. Once they'd finished, she would wrap the sheet around her body and walk to the bathroom to put on her robe. Other than that she preferred to sleep alone, and not many men invited her back to their place once they'd got what they wanted.

At Luc's house, on the other hand, she felt out of her element, so she just drank her Perrier and made small talk with her host. It was true, she agreed, that life in the countryside did seem very nice. That silence, and all the space, not to mention the greenery. The problem was she didn't think she could live out here on her own. You had to drive twenty minutes to reach the nearest supermarket, for a start. Still, it was something to think about... Luc nodded at everything she said and the conversation slowly tapered off, like a fire on an ice floe. Thankfully they started talking about little Grégory and Luc suddenly grew animated again. He knew all the details of the case too. He also loved watching the true-crime show *Faites entrer l'accusé*. As did Rose, of course! They were both compelled by that strange curiosity for everyday horror.

"I don't know what draws me to it. It's . . . beyond my control."

"Same for me," said Luc. "It's like anyone could snap and do that sort of thing."

"Exactly."

"Apparently one of my great-uncles ended up in a penal colony."

Rose brightened up. "Really?"

"Yeah. I even found some newspaper cuttings from back then. The family was almost proud of him."

After that they reeled off the names that were like passwords for crime enthusiasts. Francis Heaulme. Simone Weber. Xavier Flactif and his wife, Graziella. The Mourmelon Triangle. Marc Dutroux. Natascha Kampusch.

"Oh yes!" said Rose excitedly.

"And little Estelle."

They fell silent then, as if they'd gone too far. That little girl's face had once stared out from every shop window in the country. You would see her in butcher's shops, hairdressing salons, bus stops: the same pale skin, the same red sweater, the same dimple in her chin. Rose had wondered so many times what could have happened to that smile from twenty years ago. And to think all it took was a minute for the void to swallow up the most precious part of your existence.

"Well..."

Luc finished his Coke. He stood up now in front of her, his backlit face erased, arms dangling.

"Are you coming?" he asked.

Rose stood up in turn, smoothing down her skirt before following him into the corridor. In the darkness, Luc took her hand and she slipped off her shoes. She felt a bit idiotic. She felt young. She was happy. She squeezed his hand and he squeezed hers. She wanted the moment to last longer but she wanted to be in bed with him now; she was all over the place, just like she used to be at fifteen or at twenty. It was wonderful and unbearable. When she entered the bedroom, however, she felt abruptly disenchanted. Everything in there—the padded headboard, the rattan nightstands, the charcoal portraits on the wall—spoke of the woman who'd lived there before. It was awful.

"Carole was getting into drawing toward the end," Luc explained. "I should take all this down to the garage soon."

Not wanting to upset him, Rose said the drawings were very pretty. She noticed in passing that the artist's signature took up quite a lot of space.

Luc sat on the bed and started undoing his laces. But they were double-knotted and he was having trouble so in the end he just pulled the shoes off by the heel. Rose watched him from the doorway. There was something in this bedroom that was putting her off.

"Aren't you coming?" Luc asked.

"Yes . . ."

But she couldn't.

"We look a bit silly, don't you think?"

Luc looked around. The objects, the furniture, it had all been there so long that it had become invisible to him. He smiled then patted the duvet next to him, inviting Rose to sit down. Once she was there, he said, "I'll take you home."

"I think that would be best."

"We'll see each other again anyway."

"Of course," Rose said, with a hint of anxiety.

They had both had plenty of love affairs, one-night stands, kids, heartaches, bereavements. They were mature. But starting your fifties was like entering a strange new land. Not so long ago, anyone over fifty had been old. They could feel it in their bones—the fatigue, the chronic diseases—and they could see it in the dryness of their skin, the sparseness of their hair. A truth of that magnitude left its mark on your body. But now that families were smashed to pieces before the kids were grown up, now that life dragged on interminably, fifty loomed like a second adolescence. Luc and Rose were there, staring at each other, not knowing what do in this new age of awkwardness. They were suspicious because happiness was not something they encountered on a daily basis. Rose found him more and more handsome. She told him this. Luc didn't return the compliment, but the look in his eyes was enough.

From the very next day, Luc began picking her up after work. Rose had asked him to park a little farther away, near the sandwich shop, because she was wary of what her colleagues would think if they saw her get into Luc's enormous Audi. But the strip mall where she worked wasn't all that large, and Nadia, the HR assistant, had seen them. Rose didn't admit it, but she was actually pretty thrilled about this. Being given a ride in a Q6 was a bit like being given a promotion. Small pleasures...

"What would you like to do?" Luc asked.

"I don't know really. You can decide."

"We could go for a drink if you want."

"Sure, why not."

"Shall we go back to the Royal?"

"Oh, no. Not the Royal."

"Okay."

They wound up at Plum, a vaguely trendy place with a clientele that mixed gray-haired Casanovas wearing Stan Smith and sexy girls with bangs, smiling hipsters, and female lawyers with painted nails. Rose never went there normally, on the grounds that it was full of pretentious assholes. The truth was that the prices were prohibitive and the clientele intimidated her. Luc, however, was friends with the owner. He seemed to be friends with everyone. He ordered a beer and Rose went for a gin and tonic. It cost twelve euros and Luc didn't even blink. In fact he bought her two more. Rose loved the buzz she got from gin, especially in summer, and it wasn't long before she was feeling perfectly at home in this place that she had loathed only two hours earlier. Perched on her barstool, she took pleasure in checking out the other customers as they went to the restrooms, and laughed at the owner's jokes. He turned out to be a very nice guy. He even gave them a plate of tapas on the house.

Later, in the Audi, Rose held Luc's face in her hands and kissed him. They rushed back to her place and fucked on the bed. It wasn't great: typical drunken sex, listless and unclimactic. But at least they'd done it. Their affair had begun.

The next day, Rose was afraid that Luc wouldn't call her, but her phone rang during her lunch break. That evening she was back on her stool in Plum. Gin and tonics, smiles, whispers. They ate tapas again and the owner came over for a chat, almost exclusively with Luc. Actually, though, Rose enjoyed that role of spectator, being an extra in someone else's scene. The two men spent their time discussing people she didn't know. They talked about the money that each of them was earning, about their success and hard-luck stories, about ways they might make even more cash in the future. Rose discovered that Plum was a bit like a chamber of commerce. People went there to pass on contacts, good ideas, to negotiate potential partnerships, to keep their finger on the pulse of the market, to find out what everyone else was up to. Above all it was a giant pissing contest, a way of working out who was the smartest, the richest, who really mattered in this town. Luc seemed to have a talent for this game and Rose couldn't help feeling a sort of maternal, possessive pride in his achievements. In a way, Luc's success was also hers. It enveloped her like a sweet scent and soon she couldn't tell the difference between that pride and her desire. She held the glass in her hands and slid the straw between her lips. The gin and tonic sparkled on her tongue. Her new life was like being on vacation.

So it was that Rose, who had promised herself she would never get sucked into it again, found herself becoming part of a couple. She found comfort in their routines, someone else she could tell things to, shared meals. She started making plans for two. She rediscovered the delicate art of compromise. She learned once again how to consider another person's needs and desires. Little by little she was lured into the swindle known as dependency.

Every day Luc would call her at lunchtime or sometimes slightly later. They didn't see each other every night, but almost, and they spent their weekends together. Luc didn't have many close friends and Rose distanced herself from her own. They were happy to be alone together and their other relationships were relegated to the background. The pleasure of sharing the same opinions on almost everything—and their enjoyment of drinking—was enough for them. Rose particularly loved those long Sundays at Luc's house in the countryside, lying on a deck chair in the shade of a cherry tree, busy doing nothing but watching the contrails fade in the blue sky above. She read magazines, novels by Katherine Pancol and Jean Teulé, and smoked light cigarettes. She kept cool by drinking Orangina mixed with vodka. Luc couldn't keep still; he always had something to do around the house. She watched from a distance as he bustled around in his old white sneakers and those Lacoste polo shirts that he bought in packs of five and wore no matter what he was doing, whether it was going out for a drink or repainting the shutters. From time to time he'd come and sit near her in the grass, just long enough to drink a beer, then he'd go back to what he'd been doing. She liked to see him going about his business like that, a tall, thin figure with slightly stooped shoulders, skin tanned, pushing a lawnmower across the grass or balancing at the top of a ladder. In the evening, after taking a shower, he would join her for a couple of Mexican beers and ask her what she felt like doing.

"We could go to a restaurant," said Rose.

Or to the movie theater, or the casino, or to Plum. Whatever she suggested, Luc never said no. He paid for everything. He was silent and gentle. Together, they had a good time. They drank. They were happy.

Rose could see only one cloud on the horizon. In bed, things never went all that well. Because of the alcohol probably, but it wasn't only that. She was always understanding. She told him it didn't matter, that they'd try again tomorrow. But the next day she woke with a hangover and a dry mouth, while Luc was already up and about. In the kitchen the Nespresso machine was making its nasal trumpeting sound. She found Luc there, shaved and dressed and smelling of Vetiver.

"How did you sleep?"

"Fine."

She tried to think of a way to bring the subject up. Through the bay windows she could see the perfectly manicured lawn, the fruit trees, the flower beds, like something from an American soap opera. Luc had made her a double espresso, no sugar. Oh well, she'd talk to him about it later.

All the same, one evening when she was having drinks at Marie-Jeanne's place, she felt compelled to get it off her chest. She and Luc had been together for more than two months by then. The failures could no longer be seen as occasional blips. Things were not going well.

"So, what, you never fuck?"

"Oh, we do. It's not that ..."

"What then?"

"Come on, I don't have to draw you a picture, do I?"

"He can't get it up?"

"He can, but ... I don't know. We never go all the way to the end, if you see what I mean."

"Ah, shit."

"Yeah."

"It's a real shame, because he's got everything going for him apart from that."

"I know. It's killing me."

"Have you talked about it at least?"

"You'd think, right? But no, he never says anything. You know the type."

"Maybe it's all the drinking."

"Well, that certainly doesn't help."

Little by little the idea crept into Rose's head: she and Luc had a drinking problem. Now, for the first time in a long time, Rose could look to the future with a degree of optimism. After years of living hand to mouth, she'd found the life that she'd only ever seen before in magazines and novels. There was no way she could mess all that up for the sake of booze. In this wonderful new land, alcohol had become her bête noire. She decided to conduct an experiment.

To change things up a little, she invited Luc to eat dinner at her place. She wanted to do things properly so she took a day off—a Friday—and spent all morning cooking before visiting the hair and beauty salon. She wore a new dress for the first time, a black sleeveless number with a zipper that ran down the back. It was the end of August. She painted her nails and forced herself not to smoke too much. When Luc rang the bell, everything was ready: the mushroom risotto, Rose, the bedroom, the fruit cocktail in the fridge.

As soon as he opened the door, Luc sensed something was up. She was dressed very elegantly, wearing high heels in her own apartment. She'd lit a vanilla-scented candle. He had a bad feeling about this.

"Are we celebrating something?"

"No, nothing special. Take a seat."

Luc sat on the couch while Rose busied herself in the kitchen. He took advantage of this brief respite to look around. Everything was clean and tidy, excessively so in fact. That sort of perfection was worrying in itself. The apartment had been prepared. But for what? Thankfully there was a large green bushy plant, long past its best, just behind the TV set, which offered some contrast to the surrounding orderliness. He stood up to get a better look at it. He rubbed his thumb along the leaves' waxy surface, wondering whether Rose had gone to the trouble of dusting them. Just then, she came back from the kitchen.

"Here," she said. "I made us some fresh fruit juice."

She was holding two large glasses filled with a smooth pinkish liquid. Luc took the glass she held out to him and clinked it against hers. He took a drink. It was good. He nodded approvingly.

"What is it?"

Rose listed the fruits she'd blended to create this concoction: strawberries, guavas, oranges, kiwis, bananas, and a carrot. Plus some crushed ice.

"Is that all?"

That was all. Luc twitched, but said nothing. He let it happen. This little game continued during dinner. Not a drop of wine with their risotto. Just water and soda. Their conversation grew laborious. They both felt trapped, like two people in an elevator stuck between floors. Luc nervously swallowed mouthful after mouthful. Rose overdid the good cheer, the wide smiles. She began to wonder if she was making a big mistake.

"Is it good?"

"Yes."

"You like it?"

"Yeah, I told you."

"It's not a race, you know. Take your time."

Fork suspended in midair, Luc looked up at her. Something glimmered in his eyes, something that Rose instantly recognized. He began to chew again, his jaws rolling while he continued to stare at her. Then his gaze returned to the contents of his plate.

"I didn't mean to make you angry," said Rose.

The words came out of her mouth almost mechanically. She immediately regretted them.

Those few words brought back the memory of a thousand other meals eaten in fear of a coming storm. They reminded Rose of her father, and precarious relationships, all those men to whom she would kowtow, out of fear and instinct. Ever since she'd been a little girl she'd had to tiptoe around men and their fits of rage, the ever-present possibility of violence, their pigheaded despotism, the fragility of any happy family at the whim of the father's mood. She remembered her father smashing plates on the tiled floor because the soup was too hot. She remembered her husband who would lock himself in the garage for hours to fiddle with a car engine while she looked after the kids. And then all the others—Eric, Serge, Christian, Benoît—all those tender, intransigent men with their certainties, their tantrums... like spoiled kids, when you thought about it. All of this returned to her in waves. Her throat tightened and she dropped her silverware onto her plate. It made a harsh metallic noise as it hit the earthenware dish and Luc looked up at her again.

"Don't you think we drink enough as it is?"

"What are you talking about?"

"We're always going out for drinks. I've had enough."

"You didn't seem to hate it at the time."

"I didn't say I hated it. I just feel like something else."

"And what is it you feel like?"

Luc spat out this question as though it were a bitter pip. She had the impression that what he meant was: *What the hell do you expect?* Feeling hurt, Rose lashed out.

"Well, I'd like to be fucked properly for a start."

Luc's face crumpled as the blood drained from it. There was an unpleasant scraping noise on the kitchen floor and his chair fell backward. Luc was standing now, his lips wire-thin. He was trying to say something but his words were stuck in his throat. He had to swallow before he could get them out. "Say that again."

Rose did not look away. She thought about her purse, with the revolver inside. It was in the chest of drawers in the entrance hall. She calculated how many steps it would take her to reach it. She thought about the new life she'd been leading. She closed her eyes and sighed.

"I didn't say anything. I'm sorry."

"Never talk to me like that again," Luc said.

Once again, it was the man who had the last word. Rose's hand tensed around her fork, her knees touched under the table and she did her best to hold in the thing that was rising up inside her, stinging her nose and her eyes.

THE MEAL ENDED without a word, amid the clinical clink of silverware and crockery, then Rose took the tart out of the oven. She'd made it specially for him, a pear tart with sliced almonds. His favorite. She cut it into six equal parts and served one of them to Luc before giving herself half a slice.

They ate quickly, without any appetite. Yet the tart was delicious, the pastry thin and crunchy, the fruit velvety and sweet. They'd messed up everything; it was too late now. Rose suggested they drink some coffee in front of the television, and they sat side by side on the couch and watched the latest episode of *Survivor*. At least the contestants' lives on the screen were simple: they were stranded on a desert island but each of them had a role to play, each of them knew exactly what was at stake. Gradually Luc and Rose's animosity was dissolved in the sparkling blue lagoons. They forgot their grievances. When a curly-haired young ER doctor named Clotilde was declared the winner, Rose took the plunge.

"I'm sorry," she said. "I'm really sorry. Please forgive me."

Luc turned toward her and apologized in turn. He'd lost his temper too. Better just forget the whole thing. Amnesia is as essential as gentleness to any relationship. Love can't survive if grudges are held. Relieved, Rose decided to seal this peace treaty in time-honored fashion.

"I could get us a drink, if you like. I have some wine, or some cognac."

"I'd rather go to bed," said Luc.

"Already?"

"Yes."

"Here?"

"Of course. Why not?"

They'd never slept at her place before. Luc's house was so much more welcoming. In comparison, Rose's apartment seemed more like a pied-à-terre. Then again, Rose guessed what he had in mind. After the cheap shot she'd taken, he wanted to erase the insult, to prove her wrong. And since they hadn't drunk a single drop of alcohol, it was surely now or never.

"Okay . . . ," she said.

Before going to bed, Rose spent quite a while in the bathroom. Then, barefoot in a babydoll, she went into the bedroom to join Luc. He was waiting for her in bed, hands flat on the pink sheets. He was naked and there was a serious look on his face. She lay down next to him. On the wall facing them, family photographs told the story of her past thirty years. Luc had opened the double-glazed window and a gentle wind fluttered the tulle curtain. The city sounds in the distance were so constant that in the end they felt like silence.

"Do you want to sleep?" Rose asked.

"No."

"Maybe we should talk."

"What do you want to talk about?"

He seemed distant, as if he'd retreated behind his shell. She hardly recognized his handsome vertical face. Luc was fully focused on himself, on what he was about to do.

"Come on," he said.

"What do you mean?"

She felt a hand close around her arm and then Luc's mouth was pressed hard against hers. Their teeth clattered. Rose tensed. His hand went down between their bodies, reached between her legs. But Rose didn't want to. She held her thighs tight together. She didn't want to give in to him, to feel that weight crushing her. Too late— he was on top of her now, holding her down on her hips and her throat. He used his knee to force open her legs, and Rose closed her eyes. She knew how this would end. For a minute or two Luc huffed and puffed but nothing really happened. Soon he had to face the facts and he rolled onto the side. His face was red and he was out of breath. She had done nothing to help him.

"It happens," said Rose. "Don't worry about it."

She barely had time to glimpse it coming before Luc's hand slapped hard into her face. At first she felt only a sort of numbness, then very quickly she recognized the taste of copper in her mouth. She raised a hand to the cut in her lips. She looked at her fingers. It wasn't much: a dab of color on her fingerprints. Two drops. And the ringing feeling in her incisors. Luc was already sitting on the edge of the bed, putting on his jeans. Rose licked her lower lip with the tip of her tongue as the pain filled her head. She could feel a tiny tear in the flesh of her mouth. She sucked up the blood and got a better taste. The sensation made her think of candy: that sweet, changing flavor, the tingling of the wound. Luc put on his sneakers, then his polo shirt. In no time he was dressed. He left the room without a word. It was all so sudden that Rose was motionless for a moment, mute, incapable of thought. Sitting up in bed, she listened to the silence that filled the empty apartment. She didn't move a muscle, not even to tremble or shed a tear. Once she was sure that Luc had gone, she stood up and went to the entrance hall to get the revolver from her purse. The feel of the weapon in her hand did her so much good. Back in her bedroom, she put it on the nightstand. For a while she almost wished that Luc would come back.

TWO DAYS LATER Luc and Rose were face-to-face again.

She'd talked to Marie-Jeanne about it, though, and the two women had agreed: it was over with that bastard. In Rose's kitchen they'd shared their bad memories, quoted psychologists, cited case histories and statistics. In the end it all came down to the same thing. Men could be summed up in a few simple laws. Don't listen to them.

Don't try to change them. Or heal them. And even the gentlest man is a beast deep down, for better or worse. Violence was their common denominator.

But Luc had called Rose—on her work phone this time, so she answered without knowing who it was. Caught off guard, she'd answered yes, no, yes, trying to bring the conversation to a swift end. Except that Luc had spoken the magic words: *L'Île Sobre*.

L'Île Sobre was the best restaurant in town. A large and ancient building situated on the outskirts of Nancy, with an exceptional wine list and six pieces of silverware either side of your plate. Rose had never been there, but—like everyone else in the city—she knew the restaurant's reputation. She'd seen photographs on Facebook and had read a two-page eulogy in a local magazine. Every famous person in the region, every Ligue 2 soccer player, had been there. In the evenings, particularly, it was a renowned spot, thankfully free of those modern camouflage techniques: background music and subdued lighting. The chef, too, scorned all easy shortcuts. Instead of relying on spices and exoticism, he put his faith in the excellence of the ingredients, the science of cooking, and his own skill. At least that was what Rose had read in a blog by a *Figaro* journalist, who had been especially complimentary about the poached asparagus, the monkfish medallions, and the truffle consommé julienne. You had to book weeks in advance to get a table, unless you knew people or were willing to pay two or three hundred euros per person. Rose simply couldn't turn down this invitation to another world. You only live once, after all.

THE RESTAURANT parking lot was still mostly empty when Rose arrived in her Fiat Punto and she immediately spotted Luc's Audi. She parked at a distance and waited for him to come over to her, looking sheepish and holding a bunch of flowers.

"Good evening."

"Hi."

"You're all dressed up."

Rose didn't reply. She would have preferred not to make an effort but she'd been afraid of sticking out like a sore thumb in this high-class place that she already found slightly intimidating. So she was wearing high heels and a pretty white flower-patterned dress, and she'd spent twenty-five minutes on her bun. Luc held out the bouquet and, after a moment's hesitation, Rose took it from him. On the other hand, when he tried to kiss her on the cheek, she cut him short with a coldly raised eyebrow.

"Well, I'm glad you're here anyway," Luc said.

"I imagine you are."

"Have you been here before?"

"What do you think?"

Luc grimaced. They were off to a good start.

"It's a nice place," he said. "You'll see."

Inside, it soon became clearer why the restaurant was called The Sober Island. The inner courtyard looked a little like a cloistered garden, and in this haven of comfort her anger was blunted, deadened by the science of lighting, the heavily draped tablecloths, the perfect spacing of the tables, and the satisfying, almost musical crunch of the gravel. To loosen her up a little more, Luc ordered two glasses of champagne as soon as the waiter came over. They sipped their drinks while pretending to peruse the menu. In reality Rose was spying on the other customers, who were beginning to arrive in groups of two or three. They were mostly older people, regulars, smiling and moving slowly through this already con-quered land. Try as she might, Rose couldn't help en-vying them. She consoled herself with the thought that they would snuff it before she did. Life being what it was, however, even that wasn't sure.

Very soon their glasses were empty and Luc ordered a bottle. Out of timidity, Rose ordered the same dishes as Luc: the consommé and the rabbit stew. After that, Rose's calculated coldness gradually melted in the pleasure pro-vided by the food and drink. She was especially pleased by the efforts Luc was making to keep their conversation alive. He even talked about his sister, a subject that was normally taboo. She'd just borrowed 150 euros from him and Rose again lamented her shamelessness. Yet something was holding Luc back from saying what he needed to say. He kept circling around it and Rose was amused to see him floundering like that. Just before dessert, growing tired of his prevarications, she decided to make the first move.

"All right, listen, you didn't invite me here to talk about the weather..."

The shutters came down over Luc's face, then he lowered his eyes.

"I know I screwed up."

"And?"

The situation was becoming almost entertaining for her. She watched him struggle, guessing at the whirlwind of words and contradictions spinning away inside him, the feelings tightly wound in a ball of silence. It was almost touching. His inability to speak about it was in itself the proof that he loved her.

"Cat got your tongue?"

"What do you expect me to say?"

"Oh, not much."

The maître d' arrived just then with their sorbets. From where they sat on the patio, they could hear the clink of crockery, an occasional burst of laughter, glimpse the smooth, economical movements of the waiting staff. Their waiter uttered the words "guava juice, vacherin, and lemon curd," then Luc and Rose were left alone again.

"What do you want from me?" Luc repeated aggressively. "I don't know what to say. I'm not going to get down on my knees and beg."

Rose put a hand to her bodice. She was suddenly feverish. She'd been getting these hot flashes more and more often recently, waking up covered in sweat, her heart pounding. She took a few deep breaths and the inferno died down.

"Listen," she said, "I'm not a kid anymore. I've been through too much to let this kind of thing happen to me."

Luc nodded slightly and closed his eyes.

"I'm too old to take this crap from some loser."

"Hang on..."

"No. The problem with men like you is that you don't talk and you don't listen either. Maybe you love us. I'm watching you now, looking so unhappy, and I think: maybe that idiot does actually love me."

The insult amused Luc and his expression lightened a little.

"But what's the point? The more you love us, the worse it is. I don't want that anymore."

Luc didn't flinch, but she saw something like a breath of wind rippling across his face. Briefly a veil was lifted, just long enough for her to glimpse another face beneath it, a crumbled, childlike face that she had never seen before and that touched her heart.

"It's over," she said.

"What do you mean?"

He'd spoken too loudly, and instinctively he looked around to make sure nobody was staring at him. They weren't, of course. The other customers were calmly enjoying their meals, caught up in their own little dramas and satisfactions, which they too did their best to conceal. On the table, the sorbets were starting to melt. Rose lit a cigarette.

"I swore to myself a while ago that I wouldn't put up with this sort of thing anymore. And I'm not just going to wipe the slate clean. That would be too easy. I'm not going to forget this. And I hope, for you, that there will never be a next time."

Luc closed his eyes and nodded. Rose could have clarified her intentions with another sentence but she thought that was enough. She was reminded of the dog she'd killed with her revolver at the Royal. Well, he's been warned, she thought. She was determined this time.

Luc opened his hand on the table and their palms met. They weren't young or good-looking or even particularly happy. They did not have their whole lives ahead of them. They were a woman and a man with drinking problems and money problems, with lines on their faces and an unsatisfactory sex life, with their car keys and the pills they had to take with every meal, with their bad habits and their years of memories, unpaid bills on a chest of drawers in the entrance hall, the remote control lying on the TV guide, colored folders containing thirty years of paperwork like a summary of all their efforts. A man and a woman...What could be more banal or more necessary? A woman and a man holding hands and thinking that they understand each other. That's all it takes to make a couple.

PART THREE

ARRIVING OUTSIDE their hotel, Rose took an immediate dislike to it. Yet at first sight the place looked exactly the way she'd imagined it. And while the Q6 silently eased to a halt, she contemplated the building's endless facades and the long hedges that echoed its emerald green roofs. She counted three Porsches in the parking lot, along with two or three even flashier vehicles whose names she didn't know. She could have asked Luc, who watched a TV show about cars every Sunday morning, but she preferred to remain mute. A porter rushed out to greet them.

"Not bad, huh?" said Luc.

"It, um . . ."

While the porter took care of their luggage, Rose looked for the promised five stars but couldn't find them on the large swinging doors or on the carpet runner that swept up the stairs, nor even on the staff uniform. Apparently the Hotel Royal in Evian didn't believe it necessary to flaunt this distinction because its clientele knew what to expect anyway. As Luc waited for her at the top of the stairs, Rose did her best to hurry after him, although it wasn't easy in high heels while carrying her purse, her left wrist weighed down by the thick gold chain that Luc had given her—the souvenir of another argument.

At the reception desk the concierge confirmed their reservation: one room, three nights, with a lake view. Breakfast was served from seven till eleven. The restaurant, the bar, the gymnasium, the spa, the yoga classes. Luc asked a few questions and the concierge—a young guy with slicked-back hair who had clearly powdered his T-zone—answered them all fully. His calmness was in itself the first indication of the hotel's luxury. Despite this, Rose couldn't shake off her initial impression. Something was bothering her, but what? She didn't have time to dwell on this question. A young woman asked them to follow her. On the way to their room she showed them how to reach the various attractions that the concierge had listed. In the elevator there was a silence. The chambermaid gave Rose and Luc a suitably friendly smile as they glided upward from floor to floor, then finally broke the silence.

"Did you have a good trip?"

In truth, the five-hour drive had passed without any problems, though without any particular pleasure either. Luc and Rose were here to celebrate a sort of anniversary. Two and a half years earlier, they had met one evening at the Royal. It seemed a long time ago, almost like another world.

Occasionally, when she was taking a bath or drinking her coffee on the terrace of Luc's farmhouse, Rose would try to go back through the events that had led her to that point. But there aren't really that many events in a life. Rose had the impression that many of her choices had made themselves, almost in spite of what she herself might have thought. The logic of the daily grind had done its work and each change had occurred with her agreement, whether out of tiredness or politeness. All things considered, this law of inertia, or momentum, was enough to explain almost everything. For example, Rose couldn't have told you why she'd quit her job. It wasn't as if she'd hated it. Another ten years or so and she'd have had her full pension. Sure, her colleagues got on her nerves sometimes and she never exactly leaped out of bed in the mornings, but on the whole she'd quite liked her job. In the same way she couldn't really have explained why she'd moved in with Luc. She'd begun by sleeping there a couple of nights every week, then four or five, then all the time. Soon the simple fact of having to go home to pick up some belongings and go through her mail had seemed like a pointless chore. She was paying all those bills for nothing. The apartment was rented so all it took was a few phone calls and three letters and she was out of there, the lease terminated, her previous life erased. It had taken only half a day to move all her stuff and, standing in Luc's garage, Rose had been able to see for herself how little space her past occupied.

In the end Luc had suggested that she work for him. That way she wouldn't have to commute every day: a twenty-five-mile round trip was unnecessary, tiring, even dangerous. This seemed like a good idea and Rose was easily convinced. She set up her office on the mezzanine, with a brand-new PC, a photo of her kids, a phone line, and the philodendron that had survived from her open-space office. Disillusionment had set in quickly. In theory her job was to manage Luc's schedule, act as a liaison with service providers, take care of his accounts and paperwork . . . to be his secretary, basically. But Luc's business wasn't organized like that: it took place on his cell phone, in restaurants, on construction sites, almost in secret. It was a man's world, where Luc and his friends laughed at the same things, talked about women in the same way. And Rose was left playing solitaire on her computer for hours on end. The worst thing was that she was earning more than she had before: two thousand euros per month, all of it unofficial, a personal agreement between the two of them. She worried about her social security contributions. Luc told her it didn't matter. He was there. In that way, little by little, he convinced her to change everything. He even managed to persuade her to leave her revolver inside a trunk in the garage. She didn't need a gun anymore, now he was here. Rose let him disarm her. From time to time she would pick up her revolver and slip it into her purse for the day while she went shopping in town. It was a strange sort of compulsion. Just another way to feel a little bit free.

AT THE HOTEL ROYAL they took a brief tour of their suite, marveling at the high ceilings, the classy ambience, the dazzling white bed linen that contrasted admirably with the baroque wallpaper. There were fresh flowers on the dressing table and in the bathroom, providing a hint of spring amid all the stifling opulence. The balcony overlooked the lake. The instructions for calling room service or having your sheets changed were written in five languages.

"Look, they've even got it in Russian and Chinese," Rose said.

Luc said nothing. As always he was inspecting the finishing touches: fingering the edges of the wallpaper to check that it was properly glued down, knocking on dividing walls to gauge their solidity. From his frown, she concluded that the work was impeccable.

"So what now?" Rose asked.

She felt relatively at home in this room, but the rest of the hotel—with its endless corridors, its top-class facilities, its wealthy clientele—intimidated her. She didn't know how she was supposed to act, feared she would unwittingly break some rule of etiquette. Every step she took might end with her tripping up. Should she wear a bathrobe to go to the pool or could she walk through the hotel in her swimsuit? Surely she wasn't expected to bring her purse with her if she wanted to take a dip? She became aware that she was breathing heavily. What an idiot! It was their anniversary. They should make the most of this break. All the same she was wary of these high-society types with their icy manners.

They killed the next two hours at the spa, moving from hot to cold, from steam room to ice bath. The effect was certainly invigorating, but no amount of spa therapy could wash away Rose's unease. In the hot tub, Luc took her hand and they smiled at each other apologetically. Yet everything was perfect. They were relaxing, the weekend had just begun, and later they would eat dinner on the terrace together, whatever the price. Yes, everything was perfect and when Luc suggested they go for a little walk around the lake, Rose almost burst into tears.

Later that afternoon, however, they did go for that walk, advancing side by side, vaguely distant and yet close, bound by habit if nothing else. Summer was over and most of the tourists had left Evian; those who remained were quiet retirees, rich childless couples, and of course some local families, who were easily recognizable from their strollers, their chain-store clothes, and the way they walked as if they actually had somewhere to go. Luc and Rose watched all of this as they followed the shore of the lake, its mercury waters reflecting the immaculate blue sky. A handful of teenagers on rollerblades sped past them, brushing their shoulders, which gave rise to a discussion on education and an imagined increase in purse-snatching. In reality, though, they didn't care about any of this. They were just waiting for dinner. They still had that safe harbor of fixed hours and suitable behaviors. For Luc and Rose, alcohol remained a reliable fallback solution.

So they went to the hotel restaurant as early as possible—about seven p.m.—and ordered the rack of lamb recommended by the waiter, along with a vintage bottle of Aloxe-Corton. From the terrace of the Hotel Royal they could look out over the cold movements of the lake, its surface rippled by September shivers. Soon Rose had to cover her bare shoulders. She was in a sullen mood and complained about the slowness of the service, the dimness of the lighting. During the meal they talked about some common acquaintances. Bad-mouthing others was always practical; that way it was easy to find things to agree about. And then there was the pleasure of attacking their little idiosyncrasies, the way they brought up their kids;

pouring scorn on other people's tastes in decor or criticizing how they spent their money gave Luc and Rose a means of papering over certain cracks of their own that they preferred not to see. Naturally they started talking about Catherine, Luc's sister, and they dwelled on that subject for a while. Catherine was on a long run of bad luck and Rose never missed an opportunity to run her down. Poor Catherine lived in the countryside, in an old, renovated farmhouse, with her dogs and a strange man who sold conservatories door-to-door. Almost every day she would call Luc and she always had something to complain about. Once, the roof of their house had a leak. Another time, one of their dogs had gastric torsion. Or she might call because her boyfriend hadn't met his sales targets and they were facing bankruptcy. And then there was her hip, her neighbors, her bladder, her chickens getting eaten by a fox, and so on. Luc always listened patiently, hiding his irritation, and in the end he would offer to help her out. Catherine would protest. It would take another three phone calls to persuade her to let Luc send a check. The worst thing was that Rose had never met this perpetually troubled sister, even though she didn't live far away. Rose didn't care, but that was no reason not to complain about it.

"Anyway, at least I know where I stand with her."

"What do you mean?"

Luc knew what she was going to say, of course, and Rose herself was aware of repeating herself. Between the two of them words never resolved anything. They marked out positions. They reiterated resentments. And each subject of discussion served only to spotlight their own problems, to harp on the same sources of annoyance. That was life as a couple: this endless battle.

"Well, she's jealous, isn't she?"

"That's nonsense."

"The jealousy is killing her. It's so obvious!"

"Give it a rest."

But it was too late. The words—poisonous, always the same—burst from her mouth as if they had a life of their own, and suddenly Rose's anger was out too, like a dog straining its leash.

"She can't stand it because her life is so crappy and she lives in that shithole. She hates us because we're successful."

"*We're* successful?" Luc asked ironically.

Rose immediately felt tears blur her vision. She arched her back, doing her best to hold them in.

Once Luc had scared her. He'd hurt her. Now it was worse. He made her feel that she was dangling by a thread. Such was her dependence, so deep had she fallen into servitude, that a single word would be enough to send her spinning into the void.

For a long time she had not been able to put a name to this allusive violence. It was far from the obvious brutality of domestic abusers that you read about in the newspapers. There was no sobbing, there were no bruises. It was a violence of allusions, silences, absences. All it took was a single clash and Luc would disappear. She would be left alone for several days, with nobody to share her bed or her meals. Luc had taken her in like a stray dog. And he abandoned her like a dog too. If she ever asked him why, the wall of silence would only thicken and there was a risk that he would leave her again. After the hundredth time, unable to take it anymore, she'd pleaded: just talk to me! The only result was a slight ripple on the surface of his handsome vertical face. Several times she'd wanted to leave him but she couldn't escape; she was a prisoner in this cell of silence and comfort. All the same she wondered what could be brewing behind that face, inside this man incapable of words. She imagined storms, constricted hurricanes, a whirlwind in confinement. One day it would all have to come out. Like an idiot, she hoped it would.

She still remembered that weekend when he left her alone for the first time. They'd had an argument after dinner, because she kept leaving her purse on the chairs in the living room, which was obviously not where it belonged, or—even worse—on the bed, which was bad luck, and Luc had exited the house without a word. She'd heard him picking up his keys, the glass doors sliding open and shut, then the roar of the Q6 on the driveway. After that she didn't hear from him for two days. Not only that but Rose's car was in the garage, as if he'd planned the whole thing on purpose. Rose found herself trapped in that big house, which suddenly no longer seemed so cozy, swearing that she wouldn't just let this happen to her. But all she had done was wait for his return, pacing from room to room, from the bed to the couch, from the bathroom to the toilet, dialing numbers on her phone before abruptly hanging up. That was how she realized that she'd burned all the bridges with her old life, without ever reaching the life that Luc was leading apart from her. Now she was stranded. She had nobody.

That Saturday morning, her mouth dry from cigarettes after a restless night, Rose had decided enough was enough. After taking a shower she'd made herself a vodka and pineapple juice, for courage, and she'd drunk it while staring through the window at the frost sparkling on the short grass in the pale February sunlight. She started to feel better. Two glasses later, she called Marie-Jeanne, who said simply: "Ah, hello stranger." And then they'd talked as naturally as if nothing had ever come between them. Rose told her friend about Luc.

"You should get out of there for good," said Marie-Jeanne.

"Where am I supposed to go?"

"Just come here for a start. Come on, we'll have a laugh together."

"No. I don't have a car. Anyway, I've been drinking..."

"On your own?"

"Yeah, I know, I know, please don't start lecturing me."

"What were you drinking?"

"Vodka."

"Stay there. I'm on my way."

Rose had giggled, then quickly got dressed to welcome her friend. The two of them had stayed up late that night, drinking and talking endlessly—about men, about their kids, about work, about their electric youth, about their bodies which were falling apart, about the pain of being a woman, about hot flashes and all the rest, and then about what was on TV these days. Marie-Jeanne had a soft spot for Thierry Ardisson, whom she couldn't help finding sexy with his big hands and his old lecher's face. Rose preferred the guy from the series *Castle*. They laughed a lot that night and danced while listening to RFM's disco show on the radio, before ending up fully dressed together in the same bed. On Sunday morning, Marie-Jeanne had left with the words: "Honey, if you survive this hangover, you should get the hell out of this place and never come back."

But Rose had stayed, and on Monday, when she heard Luc's key turning in the lock, she'd hated herself for the relief she felt.

There had been other, similar episodes. Rose would have preferred it if Luc had taken mistresses. That's what she told the female shrink she went to see, although the woman seemed to be more of a hypnotist and midwife than anything else. In any case, the shrink hadn't been able to do much to help her, other than dispensing the sort of advice you could find in any women's magazine and recommending that Rose drink herbal tea. Her doctor hadn't been much more useful; he'd prescribed Effexor, but the antidepressant had just given her a bunch of side effects: dry mouth, bloating, diminished sex drive. It was during this period that Luc had changed the combination on the safe—for her protection, he said. Their worst arguments had come after he locked up her revolver, but in the end Luc had given in. "Just go ahead and off yourself, if that's what you want." In fact, though, Rose had never even thought about turning the gun on herself.

On the other hand, the idea of leaving Luc had begun to worm its way into her head. She'd warned Luc about the possibility. Each time, he just ignored her, cutting the conversation short with a word or a curt wave of the hand. Rose was getting all worked up over nothing. He would never let her ruin everything. And that *never* was like a wall. Luc wasn't joking.

From then on, Rose took to regularly checking that the revolver was still inside the safe. One day, she thought, it might be her way out. She also feared that it would end up in Luc's hands. Gradually, day by day, she was preparing for violence.

Despite all this, she would sometimes feel surprised, for example when she saw Luc from behind, doing the cooking, his sleeves rolled up, or when she watched him on the phone, talking with a plumber or a bricklayer, or when his figure suddenly appeared in a doorway. When a smile revealed his crooked incisor. She couldn't imagine herself without him and she grew angry at herself for not being able to resolve this equation of hatred and attachment.

MEANWHILE, on the terrace of the Hotel Royal, the temperature was dropping quickly. Rose tightened her grip on the stole that covered her shoulders. She looked at the chain around her wrist. Her beautiful Hermès watch. That 102-euro bottle of wine.

"We should separate," she said.

Luc sighed and rolled his eyes.

"I'm not joking," said Rose.

"You don't know what you're saying."

"I'm going to leave you. I've had enough. There's no point going on like this."

"And where would you go? What would you do?"

"I'd figure something out."

"You don't even have a bed to sleep in."

"I'd manage. How did I cope before I met you?"

"Exactly. You weren't managing all that well, were you?"

Farther off, a waiter was moving from table to table, lighting candles. Two by two, the customers' faces lit up and came suddenly into focus, and their conversations began again, with revived enthusiasm. The quietness of the terrace was punctuated in this way by talkative masks, animated by the flickering of the flames, which seemed to sharpen the cold wind blowing in from the east. Luc put his sweater on. With his hair sticking up, a yellow reflection glowing in his pupils, he said: "You're talking nonsense. I don't want to hear any more about this."

But Rose was determined.

That night, for the first time in ages, they fucked. It was almost somnambulistic. They were lying down and Luc's hand touched Rose's hip. They hugged and she felt him hard against her, so she urged him in. She was afraid it wouldn't last. He penetrated her quickly and she felt it: that old frisson. She'd always thought that was the best part of sex, the very first thrust, when a man's cock went deep inside her. Luc lay on top of her for a moment, whispering words into her ear, words she wasn't sure she really understood. But from his intonation, she guessed at affection, regret. Gradually Luc's erection softened. She held him tight.

"It doesn't matter," she said. "We'll try again tomorrow."

Luc fell onto the side. He hadn't come, and neither had she. You could barely even call it sex. He fell asleep almost straightaway and Rose went to the bathroom. She was surprised by her reflection in the mirror, but this time not in a negative way. Instead of ruing the lines on her face, she was amazed by how alive she looked, braced against the passing of time, still beautiful despite the weight of the years. She examined herself for a long time, noticing how well she took care of herself, the elegance of her fingernails, the exactness of the lipstick on her lips, the tenacity she put into existing despite this man who didn't deserve her.

All her life, men had ruined everything for her. Boyfriends who let her down, a husband who yelled at her, children who kept her awake at night, bosses who interrupted her, colleagues trying it on, the lechers and the shy ones, a drink in the evening and Sundays in bed, the whole array of boys that had been her audience, her horizon. She'd wanted their love, their protection. She'd wanted to escape them. But it was her drug; it was there, under her skin, built-in unhappiness. Thinking this, she felt suddenly, deeply sad.

On the other side of the door was Luc's body, asleep, already old. She could hear his regular breathing and she resented the miserable way they were using their last sparks of vitality. One day nothing would remain in the mirror but the promise of death and her regret that she hadn't done more with her life. Looking back over all those men, all those failed relationships, she came to one conclusion. She should never have loved them as much as she did.

She opened the bathroom door and went back into the bedroom. She was going to pack her bag and escape while Luc was asleep. At worst, if she woke him, she'd scream and the hotel staff would come to her rescue. Her hands were trembling with euphoria and fear, but she felt certain that this five-star hotel offered her the infallible protection of its good manners, its bespoke service, the ideal aid of its chandeliers and its bucolic views. In such a setting, violence was impossible, her revolver unnecessary. She was saved.

Her thoughts went no further. Two bullets from the .38 penetrated her chest, perforating the aorta and the heart, expelling a cloud of blood and flesh, a powder of bones that stained the white carpet, the green velvet wallpaper.

Arm outstretched, gun in hand, Luc had just purged fifty years of silence. The liquid gleam in his eyes spoke for him. There would be no other explanation.

Nicolas Mathieu was born in Épinal, France, in 1978. His first novel, *Aux animaux la guerre*, was published in 2014 and adapted for television by Alain Tasma in 2018. He received the Prix Goncourt, France's most prestigious literary award, in 2018 for his second novel, *And Their Children After Them* (Other Press, 2020). He lives in Nancy.

Sam Taylor has translated more than sixty books from French, including Laurent Binet's *HHhH* and Leila Slimani's *The Perfect Nanny*, and his four novels have been translated into ten languages. He was born in England, spent ten years in France, and now lives in the United States.